MARA

ALEXANDRA ELKHOURY

M
A
R
A

SPRING CEDARS

Copyright © 2025 by Alexandra Elkhoury

All rights reserved

First edition, 2025

Cover art by Rami Tannous
Book design by Spring Cedars

ISBN 978-1-963117-42-4 (paperback)
ISBN 978-1-963117-43-1 (hardback)
ISBN 978-1-963117-44-8 (ebook)

Published by Spring Cedars
Denver, Colorado
www.springcedars.com

This book is dedicated to Therese Sansour,
my late great-aunt who inspired me to start writing.

TABLE OF CONTENTS

PROLOGUE

My soul was bound to a greater power no one had met before. To some, it was gentle, caring, and seducing in the utmost tranquility; however, it made me hurt in a way no one else could understand or withstand. An everlasting brainwash that caused me to commit my worst mistakes. I prayed for moments of peace, yet they never came to exist. I felt the eternal woe of a wounded lamb who continued to live and die by the eyes of a thousand predators. I remained alone and unable to escape. That power had many names. To some a blessing, to others a curse. In my case, a downfall that took my freedom.

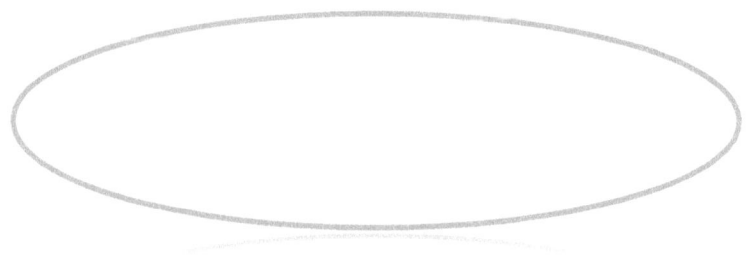

PART ONE

CHAPTER 1

On a rural farm in the town of Ranches, a corpse took life by the name of Mara. The estate provided everything she could ever need to survive, but her will to survive was yet to be fulfilled. Mara never wished for money, nor did she care for material possessions. Rather, she was fascinated with the meaning of existence and thoughts. She was frightened by the possibility of living in the dismal aura of people who never seemed to understand her. All mental, of course. As it always was.

Solitude called her. But it was an excuse to escape relationships and love, sins that attempted to conquer her daydreams. She lay motionless within the dark walls of her bedroom, engulfed in hellish stillness. With her eyes closed, she observed the various pathways of the soul. What she perceived as her own inner being, was not always real, for she was often blinded by physical pain. But Mara did not care about what had been done to her temporary body, only the cerebral consequences.

Mara had been collared at a young age. On the farm, she had found solace through Hemingway and the other animals. She was just like them. A creature. Mara's limbs were weak from constant labor, her mind and irises too. She was covered in scars, reminders of her horrific past. *I do not hold any joy labeling myself as part of mankind. I do not wish for comparison, judgement, competition, or jealousy. I want peace.*

CHAPTER 2

Ten years ago, Mara was wandering through the hallway by the kitchen with Hemingway. Her heart pounded joyfully, as would any other little kid's. The time struck four when Father and Mother returned. Neither had taken on their parental roles, as Mara would soon find out. Violent flames burned within their pupils, bringing a harsh warmth to the room. Mother kept throwing attacks, while Father stood still, eyes sorrowful yet immaculate. He was raised on the farm, and though there were many things he wished to see in the world, he was never able to leave. Those born in Ranches could never escape. They relived the same day over and over again. Sometimes, they would talk about leaving, but no one ever followed through with it. Father married Mother as alcohol alone could no longer fill the hole in his heart. But he always thought of what could have been. Mara knew he regretted settling down. A happy home, there was none. A happy family, not to be seen either. Mara knew she was destined to fail.

One day, Father fell to the kitchen tile floor with a bullet through his head. Mother stood puzzled by the gruesome event that had just occurred, gun in hand. Did Mara understand? Surely not. Her soul had not even begun to comprehend the utmost hell in which she lived. *At an early age, I had learned to believe there was no afterlife. I was already living in hell.*

Mara hid trembling in a corner while the woman scrubbed the crimson evidence from the tiles and moved on with her daily chores. The child returned to her solemn bedroom. The walls were deep emerald as was the majority of the house. Ants and roaches came through the holes in the floor to comfort the child. She was afraid of the woman who had committed the crime. A crime that was made to seem like an ordinary act, like trashing the pit of a fruit. *But a pit still has life. It can be planted, it can grow into a tree, it can provide ongoing sustenance. I wish never to give birth to dreadful human life destined to die by its own hands. Why should I bring about a side of selfishness and mistreatment that only causes more pain? Never shall my conscience wish to see such a horrific event.*

The woman had always been deranged. Father—the man who protected Mara and whom she protected—had disappeared. Who was left to understand her? Who would she care for? What was her purpose?

That night, Mara slept with a candle burning beside her. Its flames illuminated the open window, as darkness invaded the interior of the house. Even as the years went on, waking up every day reminded her of her reality. It was not the death of Father that disturbed Mara, but rather her own. She had not mourned the loss, for she had already lost by being born. *My heart never understood love. But sometimes I wish I knew how to feel.*

Chains hung from her bedroom's ceiling, dating back to when pigs and goats would be slaughtered. Therefore, Mara's dear Hemingway was unwelcome, spared from having his innocence slayed. Hemingway was only a buckling, with elongated ears pointing sideways, revealing a raw pink. Tsk, tsk, exposed he was. The door to the abattoir was never left ajar, for trust, respect, and patience with the woman were never there. Certainly a result of the woman's very own abuse as a child. An inherited trait. *I forgive Mother, each time, for having beat me, for having instilled wrongful mentalities, for having lacked love and all things beautiful, for having deserted me hungry in vengeful and childish manners, and for more. But I hold on to the hate within. It gives me an excuse to discard others without guilt. Those who attempt to break through will be shattered.*

The woman sat on the countertop, gazing at the sink, contemplating her emotions, unaware of her child's presence. At the sound of Mara's seat moving, she spun around, reconnecting with reality for a short second, then regressed into her thoughts. Alive with no feeling. Alive with no humanity. Just like Mara. Mara had grasped onto the beauty of a father who cared for her ever so slightly, but he was now gone.

"Where is Father?" Mara almost regretted uttering the words.

The woman's eyebrows shot up. She tapped her toes against the tile floor. Mother ignored the truth, for she had pushed aside the events that had occurred the night before. She arranged a basket of breads—the centers perfectly raw—and handed it to Mara. Bringing fresh bread and coffee to Mr. Bartholomew was a daily task that only a woman was born to fulfill. And it was a race. A competition. Girls her age had already begun the jealous search for men. But Mara? No, Mara craved something different. She craved freedom and adventure. Nonetheless, she ran to Mr. Bartholomew's cafe before its rotten doors opened for the day.

He glanced at her and yelled, "A female must understand the proper etiquette that is required of her. If not, she is worse than the servants whose lives are owned by others. Dirty, filthy creatures who have no use but of labor."

Why must I disregard my internal thoughts, put on a face, and please those who are set on seeing women as such? I feel the truth ignite every nerve within my body, because I know it is not right, but then again, what is wrong from right?

Mara handed Mr. Bartholomew the pile of dough and strolled toward the trash bins behind the cafe. It was a two story building. The top floor had outdoor seating with a panoramic view of the town's main square. The bottom floor was a private space where Mr. Bartholomew lived with his son and wife. The woman ceaselessly cleaned the cafe and took responsibility for her husband's drunken behavior. *Women are treated as inferior, and by doing so, assume their roles as servants. Is superiority determined by the slight difference in genitalia? Nonsense.*

As the sun began to show noon, Mara turned the page of her journal and scribbled some more. Her back pressed against the empty trash bins, creating a painful warmth. *Fulfillment comes from how close one can approach hell without falling into the devil's chains.*

Mara enjoyed gazing at her journal without someone else gazing at her with judgment. Just as she preferred spending nights rereading classics with a flashlight as opposed to conversing with others. She enjoyed literature more than real life experiences, only because it was a way to enter another's mind and interact with different perceptions. *Art is expression. Literature expresses true emotions which one can relate to, it is free from Pandora's judgment. Language is not a question of right or wrong, but rather, what one perceives as wrong or right. Communication never grazes against the terrorizing boundary of understanding. But do we ever truly understand things until we experience them on our own?*

Mara brought her journal wherever she went, as though it were another limb, whether it be to the market or two feet away from her bedroom. Through it, she could speak directly to a partner who would never judge. A partner she would never actually meet, but a partner who allowed her to be.

Mr. Bartholomew summoned her, as if he was the voice of God, and Mara felt forced to approach. He smacked her shoulders, straightening her spine, just as his son entered. He was a mere three years older than Mara and wore a long-sleeve, white, button-up shirt with beige slacks. His slicked back hair matched his defined features and black eyes. They rarely saw each other, for he spent most of his time in the city beyond Ranches, gathering provisions for his father's cafe. Mara pondered gratefully at the idea of stepping outside to explore foreign terrain. Would it be possible to escape this gloomy town and pursue the fallen aspirations of her deceased father?

CHAPTER 3

From a young age, I had been petrified at the thought of falling behind and feeling a need to prove myself to others, or those I wanted to impress would never see the talent I saw in myself.

At the break of dawn, Mara sat outside on the front porch, for she could not tolerate being near the murderer inside. The previous night, the woman was questioning herself, wondering why she had not heard back from Father. Mara already knew the truth but wished not to say it aloud for fear it would become real. When the woman was in the shower, Mara rummaged through her father's drawer and pocketed his stash of money. The following shipment of farm supplies would arrive in the morning, and Mara planned to run with it.

The sound of an engine awoke her. She had fallen asleep on the welcome mat, exhausted from attempting to break free from actuality. The image of her father shaking her shoulders brought her back to consciousness, and she stood. As the driver unloaded the farm supplies and brought them behind the barn, Mara snuck into the back of the truck and hid under a black tarp. Soon she was led away from the woman, beyond Ranches, into the unknown. Mara cradled a novel and her journal. She had always hoped for a better family, imagining other mothers at the market, walking with their children, buying groceries and toys. Plush elephants and dala horses; they would be in one hand as ice cream dripped down the other.

They had been on the road for over five hours, taking occasional breaks. Mara kept good cover. The driver failed to ever notice her. Her plan was to spend a few nights in the next town and while she did not know what to expect, she felt a sense of relief.

The town appeared deserted, mankind hid from the world, afraid to make the slightest movement, afraid to face their own. *People gossip and wonder if I have ever managed a smile. What is there to smile about? Why should I show happiness when all is not right with the world? Not one of us deserves life, so is life a punishment? Earth is hell itself. I do not know what to believe in, but I often use Christ as a tool when needed. It is hypocritical to have faith only when all else fails, but why not have something to resort to? Sure, I believe in the idea of religion; I wear a cross around my neck, like a chained animal. But then again, how can I trust in something that is so far away from me?*

The truck slowed to a stop, and the driver turned off the engine. Mara waited, pondering what it would be like to enter a restaurant full of strangers.

CHAPTER 4

Mara stood at the corner of a busy street with bright signs flickering "Ordell's Pharmacy." The lights seemed to signal the start of something new. There was so much for her to discover beyond the secluded farm. She had only been able to comprehend the world through her books. She tightened her grip on her bag which held basic toiletries, enough clothes to support a day's mere change, the novel, and her journal. Her family was very small and held almost no income, for there was nothing they truly needed to buy. Everything was there. Animals, crops, and streams of water served as their eternal sustenance. It was Father, Mother, and Mara. What more could there be?

When she began school, Mara had a few friends, until she realized that life was a game. *For me it is an easy game; I keep many people around me, but at a distance. If one person gets too close with greed, I desert them. With no feeling in mind. I have no emotion. Rather than allowing the horrors of this game break me, I ally myself with them.* Just before the end of elementary school, Mara's parents took her out, because school had no purpose for a drunkard and a mentally ill.

Standing alone on the busy corner, she was now in charge of finding her own shelter. It was overwhelming, and she felt insignificant among the herd of people and cars. *Shocking, it is as though modernization is based on the need for distance, a direct separation of nature and man. However, there is also a separation of man and man. All walk in unison, yet all remain detached. They disregard humanity's intricate links, subconsciously fearing its control, and continue to isolate themselves from further human contact. I wonder if they ever yearn to reach out and touch one another. To feel the warmth. To be close.*

Mara found a motel across the street and entered. A man behind the reception desk was asleep in his chair, disciplined enough to make money, yet disconnected from his body to achieve it at all. Various shades of paint decorated the walls, and a beautiful lime fragrance carried its strength throughout the lobby. There was a hint of optimism that could never be found back in Ranches.

A breeze blew through the open front door and whispered into Mara's ear. It was Father prompting her to greet the receptionist. Near the verge of spiritual illumination—half awake, half asleep—the man struggled to form words, yet Mara understood him perfectly well. He gave her keys and accompanied her to the room. Inside, a small window framed the promising outdoors. *The morning waits for me, but the moon wishes for me to spend the night with her.* Mara drifted to sleep.

A vast forest of trees hovering above a glimmering lake appeared before her, and behind, a dirt path led to a church adorned with flowers. Mara limped to the building, her body numb. Perhaps it was guilt that dragged her away from the lake and trees toward the concrete religious site. Or perhaps it was a sense of hope. *There are answers to problems, except when there are none. Nothing is certain in this world, everything is riddled with doubt. And with every step taken toward reconciliation, there is dishonesty. Religion, or any other kind of hope, is used as an excuse in times of crisis and wrongdoing. Some people pray each night because it gives them a reason to live. Others don't have the energy to keep searching for something that may not exist. However, in the end, everyone still lacks something. And we don't even know what it is.*

Late nights, Mara would stare at her ceiling with a glimpse of motivation to become someone in the world. To stand out from the others. Until that vision was greeted by a sense of urgency, a timer. *It is easy to dream, but one must set their plan in motion instead of relishing in delusion. We are all the same, competing for this desired illusion of greatness.* Other times, Mara would look at the chains on her ceiling wanting to distance herself from the world. To become a spectator.

She sat cross-legged on the steps that led into the abandoned church. Mara was not to enter—she was not worthy enough to enter such a sacred place—but she hoped that one day she could. While she did not owe anyone anything and wished not to, she often wondered if she would ever grow to love. If a man tried exceptionally hard for her, maybe she could do the same for him. *Yet it is not simply a matter of giving and receiving. Life is a complicated game of luck. Many say the past is in the past, but I think it builds the future. Everything one goes through is what they are composed to be. The greatest part about life is that we are able to think freely; the mind cannot be chained. And that is how I survive.*

Mara continued to scribble in her journal. It was easier to write her problems where no one could judge her. *I know I have my faults, but it hurts me when people criticize them, so I try to fix them myself before they can be noticed. Throughout my shallow years, I have created an alias. A second skin, protecting me from the outside world. Judge my exterior, have at it. My mind is mine alone. Sure, there is pain in solitude, but I hold no one else to heart. And no one has ever attempted to truly discover what lies underneath my second skin. That monstrosity is only mine to know. If that special someone ever reveals themselves, I will wish the boundaries between my alias and inner self never blend, for how, then, could I ever explain to them the truth in my soul when I have lost it?*

The sun released a scorching heat, as though it were angry. *I am not exceptional, I am not intelligent nor wise, I do not advocate for anything, and I answer questions through the words of those more knowledgeable than me, but still I desire to be it all. How can I possibly accomplish everything when there is such limited time and nothing that defines me?*

Mara returned to consciousness; however, she was still not awake. It was nearly midnight as depicted on the clock beside her bed. The motel room colors matched the outdoors: entirely gray with flashes of white. It was raining, and each lightning strike disrupted space and time. Mara sat at the wooden desk across from the bed and dove back into her journal. *Thunder crashes, igniting the possibility of teleportation away from this miserable world. Sure, I could go, but I cannot think of leaving this Earth without having tried to become something great. Everyone desires a legacy. The two that raised me leave a terrible legacy, they would never become the parents I dreamed of. Father, although he tried his best, cared only about his bottle. And Mother, well, the largest part of me wishes to never see Mother again.*

Mara's hand formed cursive loops along the smooth paper. The clock ticked. *How time works in mystical ways. One thirty-two. One fifty-five. Two seventeen. Two forty-two…*

Lights flicker, and I move closer to him. There are sounds of a child crying, and I try to get up, but I am chained to a chair. The shackles around my legs cut through my skin each time I attempt to fight them. My lips quiver, and the heat from my forehead becomes rage. A judge observes me as though I am a psychopath. I beg, plead, slam my fists onto the table before me, nails digging into my palms. There are red marks alarming my nervous system of the pain, but I cannot comprehend any of it. A clock on the wall ticks valiantly. Give me a second or two, to pause this game of life so as to understand where I went wrong. One minute! Leave me be! Mara, where did you go? I am in need of your courage that formed itself in the eye of misery. To where have you disappeared all these years? Motionless and innocent are your eyes. Childish little girl. I will confide in you the biggest secret of what you will come to do...but deep within, I have no sense of warning great enough to cease you from committing it.

"Hello? Is someone there?"

The stranger's voice made Mara uneasy, awakening her from another version of a nightmare. But his trembling voice elicited a sort of pity. Mara felt his presence shift behind the motel room door. *I never can explain the difference between the monsters in one's mind and those who live in the physical world.*

Her left cheek had melted onto the desk, and the subsequent large red mark left her raw and exposed like a shaved lamb. She quickly stood with an air of confidence and opened the door.

"Did I scare you?" The man chuckled. "I'm sorry to be a disturbance. My friend runs the place, and I tend to stay in this specific room when I'm visiting. I left a few things last time."

Mara reassured him that it was not a problem, before questioning him on his travels. She wondered how people lived in this area.

"I spend most of my days on the road, attempting to experience different places and lifestyles. I'm running from the monotonous nine-to-five job. Income is not what I'm chasing—"

"Humans work hard to create a home, yet they consistently part with it for the thrill of change, how ironic," Mara interrupted.

"I kind of do as I please, and as a sort of bonus, I gain something special. Or perhaps, it is losing my family in a disturbing way that has me running. I no longer have a place to call my home. Sometimes, I do miss being anchored in a community, having familiar neighbors to share a drink with and reminisce. I might look young, but I have done a lot. We are timed by how much we have done, not by what we have done, and the clock seems to reset every twenty-four hours, you know? What was celebrated yesterday is of no importance today. Then, we are forced to recount our actions and held guilty by our minds if we fail to come out successful. A success determined not by our personal happiness, but by the societal norms we fall victim to."

He continued on, and on, and on. The storm outside had drifted into madness, and the two strangers were held hostage by the warm room. The man, named Camber, wrenched a novel out of his back pocket. He was wearing an unbuttoned blue shirt and matching shorts that fell right above his knees. His moccasins were made of leather. His copper eyes revealed hardship.

"Do you write?" Mara asked. She noticed one of the items he retrieved from the room was a journal.

He nodded his head.

"The weather is not the nicest outside, would you like to stay for a while? I would love to hear some of your writing as well, if you don't mind."

Camber smiled and began to read out loud. "Thunder strikes upon the visage of a middle-aged woman. Her reflection resembles that of the forgotten who now lay beneath soil. She tiptoes toward the hollowed grave where lies the sole promise of humankind. Death. The clock strikes twelve as to mock the common phrase, yet nothing of the sort is ordinary nor expected. Another flash bursts onto another family member, a loved one. However, it is not sorrow that floods the soul, no. Hate, rage, rebellion, and revenge are the emotions that engulf the soul, until they cause one's own downfall. I will resort to my path of silence, solitude, and mimpathy."

CHAPTER 5

Camber had experienced the trauma of losing the love of family. He suffered without it. Mara, on the other hand, suffered from never having experienced the love of family, a congenital loss.

His parents were the image of true love. They raised him in a home of compassion and gentleness. His mother was diagnosed with a chronic illness, and it took a toll on the family. His father consumed all his energy for months beside her, attending to her every need. He would greet her with smiles and sob in private. Camber witnessed his father slowly die alongside her. The day she passed, there was a silence that never left the house. Camber's father was never again the same, and he passed away shortly thereafter.

Mara remained quiet. Was it even possible to say anything after Camber's horrific tale? Something within her changed. *Poison. Extending its liquid branches into my brain. Reviving past events, summarizing how I sprouted to become who I am. There are many things that can be accomplished in life, but overcoming fate is not an easy one. One must treat others with respect in order to remain guiltless if anything bad should happen. Guilt and regret are not to be played with. It is not love but fear of lifelong regret that eats me.*

The bed Camber sat on summoned an eerie energy; however, deep inside, Mara pitied it. An object so harmless yet under constant distress. How long before it would totally collapse? How long before it would be left alone to rot? She, too, feared the idea of being left alone.

Camber scowled at the window. It seemed he was battling a war between a storm of sadness and pride. To Mara, it would build up and destroy him in the end. "You know," she said, "I only ever read stories of families like yours and always believed them to be exaggerated. My family was not the same."

He turned around, interested. "How come?"

And so Mara proceeded to tell him about her past, her mother and father, her town of Ranches, and her goat. She thought back to Hemingway. Was he okay? Then she started to hear familiar cries...from where did she remember them?

CHAPTER 6

"Mother, where did you go? It's dark here. Father? I'm scared, and the shadows are all I see. I'm scared to be alone. Please, what did I do? I'm sorry, I'm so sorry!" Hours passed. She couldn't see anything. "Where did you go?" Mara whispered. "I love you." Although she knew her mother could care less of her existence, she clung onto any hope of love. And Father, while meaning well, was a slave to Mother's word. "Please, don't leave me! Please! Please…please."

Images formed in Mara's eyes, but there was nothing there. There was no one. Once again, she had been abandoned in the night, never of importance to anyone, always left behind. Then, she felt the presence of rodents. Rather than be terrified, Mara felt comfort. These creatures had chosen to stay and keep her company. Together, the outcasts of the world could possibly find peace in unity.

Maybe Mother and Father were being cruel to be kind. Of course they were, they were her parents after all, they meant well. The darkness continued to overwhelm, and Mara continued to sit awake, alone. Another hour, another day, a week. *Perhaps one fears the darkness not for the creatures that lurk outside, but for those that haunt from within. The world is a cold place. If everyone's deepest thoughts are shared and, by chance, we all think alike regardless of our outer aliases, the world could be a warmer place. But no one's exterior matches their interior exactly. At night, the voices in our cerebrum get louder, reminding us of our countless flaws and mistakes. Tears are made to doubt our importance, and their salt serves to keep us unsatisfied with our feeble lives. Each time we attempt to quench our thirst with purity and positivity, the salt prohibits us. But it isn't happiness we long to find. We intentionally shatter ourselves so that we may piece back together in a new way, with the hope of finding true completeness. Completeness differs from happiness. We dehumanize ourselves and rely on others' satisfaction and proximity to get the high of happiness. We are carried on by a drug, that is; happiness will never be reached without another to lead the way. And that is how slowly, we lose ourselves, we start to hate life itself. When everything has been squeezed out and all you are is a vacant body.*

Mara finished recounting her life story. Although Camber remained silent, it was obvious he was processing the new influx of information. After a few seconds, he invited her on a stroll outside to get some fresh air. She agreed. So they began to walk around the motel, arrived at a deserted parking lot, and sat on a curb in silence once more. Mara went along with Camber's mood and mannerisms so as not to disturb him. The rain continued to pour, but they did not realize it, for everything was concealed by the noise of nothing. *Once you empathize with various feelings, it is easy to know when someone else develops one of those feelings. While emotions can be hidden, some people proclaim they should always be shared. However, it is not that easy nor does it always make one feel better. There were times my mouth exposed my secrets, and I regretted it instantly.* Camber's emotions were an open-book. Mara could tell that whatever was currently passing through his mind was sickening him as it had erased all pigment from his face. For Mara? Well, she was much harder to read. Tears dripped within her body, never escaping into the outer world. Darker grayness settled around them. Mara moved closer to Camber and gently put her head on his shoulder.

CHAPTER 7

Mara insisted on remaining beside Camber and accompanying him on his spontaneous adventures. What did she have to lose? Nothing. But she did have a lot to gain. Experience, freedom, and someone with whom to share the two.

After wandering aimlessly around the area, Camber proposed to take a drive. It was fascinating to analyze him. If one looked close enough, it would be clear that Camber ran from the pain of his past. He had not sat with it a moment, conversed with it, forgave it. That was all Mara was able to do in her hometown. So much so that she eventually became one with it, and everything turned into a blended confusion. What was she truly upset about? Who? It dulled any emotion and amplified the numbness. Feelings were too complicated.

Camber had one hand on the steering wheel, the other gripped a cigarette. His car had rusted paint on the outside and hoary seats on the inside. The music playing on the radio reminded Mara of her childhood, instilling a sense of rage. *A young female cries out loud but is never heard by those who are assigned to be listening.*

They were driving in the countryside, up and down the pastel-colored hills. In the sky, birds glided together in a V shape. *It makes me wonder: what does it take to be commander of the formation? Leading the others to their destination. What does it take to fit in one by one, in a congenital motion? Or is it completely innate?*

As a child, Mara would sit in the grass beside the farmhouse, playing with ants. They either followed one another in line or went their separate ways, never knowing who was to die and when. She had never seen an ant give birth before. Where was their Queen Ant? She would search and search. *Every group has a leader who is superior, propelling their species to live on. At the base is competition, where relationships are not always friendly nor understood. These relations may seem perfect from the outside, but from the inside much less. Who knows what each individual might be thinking. In the most difficult situations, only the wisest can keep their calm, they climb up the ladder by proving their worth discreetly. One of man's greatest traits: silence. But I do not believe it is the case in every situation. Silence is a beneficial act, sure, but it restricts many crucial voices that should be heard. Especially when great injustice is present. Mostly judgment directed toward race, ethnicity, gender, sexuality... Goodness! What is so pleasing about judgment? Should people be forced to think of themselves as lower than another because of the stereotypes placed upon them? Their physical appearance, their scars, their bodies...*

Gaggles of Egyptian geese—more like lovers—would wander around the farm. Mara observed in amazement, as a pair eventually had goslings, raised them, and continued to care for them. They honked when anyone approached and lived a simple life full of love, security, and family. Lovers destined to be together. *Something many humans forget. Many wish for sex only, praising its temporary pleasures and forgetting the beautiful long-term result it may forge. To place a life on this earth! A life to carry on the name, appearance, and uniqueness of a story.*

Why search for never-ending pleasures when rarity is what makes a pleasurable experience last forever?

Mara scribbled in her wrinkled journal.

Destruction of the sympathetic calm
Relinquishes a useless endorphin
Entangling the veins within a solemn corpse
Until choked and drained of its joy
Purposeless and inadequate thoughts
Are the fatalities caused by temporary pleasure
I'd wish to write a novel
Compose a musical piece
Earn talent while cruising on a wooden board
Paint the utmost wonders
Play for the finest of man
Yet the hope of it all seems draining
When action cannot be put into place
For time and effort create the basis of responsibility
However patience passion willpower drive
Come in random spurs of nothing.
-M

A solemn vérité withdraws my cry
As faded raindrops begin to flood

Their color once translucent surrenders
A disdainful pleasure of mine ears
Armies attack as long enemies
Releasing aged anger into the trenches
Collapsing while they glide through my cerebrum
Inside a shaded room I listen
Attentively their misery amuses and inhabits
Double-edged in the eyes of the audience
Immaculate liquid or spouting crimson
My borrowed eyes have failed to understand
For sight is but useless in my cave
Sounds keep me awake as if duty was to lay
Motionless only between covers
Wrapped and prepared for a fatality
Perfect in sync with the rhythmic drops
We cover for each other
-M

There is a time when hurt relinquishes immense hatred. Pure demise becomes the source of another consequence. Where one attempts to release control; however, by doing so forcefully, without patience, brings about a greater evil. An everlasting scar. Maybe it grows into an infection. Nevertheless, this scar needs not a cloak, for it has figured out its purpose. It is a sign of past catastrophes. Its strength teaches one to remember the consequences of choosing one path over another. Many hold their faith in eternal words, undying, unrequited, unconditional love. Yet we are all mere mortals, powerless to something greater.

I am a frail corpse. I live alone in a house of three. Animals wandering all about. Plants grow their roots within the palms of my body. The soul that haunts me wishes not for me to see beauty, but rather withered joys. What has been taken away from me is all that I care for, yet I did not care for it when it lay in my possession. It is the end of the world. My world. I wish not for the momentary reliefs nor the silence requited to my obvious mental torment. Of course I wish not to be bothered. But I am a sociopath, a psychopath. A misfit. Unusual and determined to remain banned from the apparent normality. Oh, well. Who would prefer an infinite bliss over eternal misery? Not I! A fictitious truth is released from my pen...

Mara gazed at her writings, contemplating the ride toward her past. It consisted of the lessons which gave her a gradual understanding of the processes of the world, helping to better her moral compass. It was her life vest.

CHAPTER 8

His hand slid onto her shoulder whenever attempting to catch her attention to point something out. The sun would glare into Mara's irises every now and then, forcing her to turn and face him. He would gift her a smile each time he noticed. *Sometimes, the past causes damage. I am not great at offering reassurance or words of wisdom. But there is never a true answer to any emotion or reaction. It is possible for an innocent interaction to spark a fuse in someone, causing new damage to their unhealed hurt, it's a chain reaction. The root will never be found. One can fall down a rabbit hole asking questions and never know the true answer. Why did she act the way she did? Even she does not truly know. Start from one question and leapfrog onto the other; small lily pads with violet flowers centered and isolated from the world, floating, stranded. It's a beautiful thing, the ability to remain curious. Life is already so difficult, and it is even harder when you believe there is no one that could ever understand the way you think. Us humans view things in various ways. The closest we can ever get to an answer is by analyzing it through multiple perspectives; but even then, what good does that do?*

The quiet remains my only companion
As my scorching anger reveals itself
Bringing about a rebellion
Scarring the tissue within my soul
A new demon sprouts
Strangling my greater good
Hell ceases to amaze me
For I've never seen anything other than its grasp
I have no reason to live yet the devil keeps me alive
Why me?
Please release me
Allow me to pull myself toward the cliffs
-M

CHAPTER 9

The pair decided to rest for the night before continuing onward with their journey. Camber found a snug motel where they slept in two beds separated by a shared nightstand.

Unlike these motels, Mara's home was very simple, with nothing more than a mattress to sleep on. *What is the purpose in having, for example, more than one TV in the house? What sort of disease would handicap a healthy man from walking a few steps to the living room? Life disintegrates before me, why should I not appreciate it as it comes? Those who rely on escapes have never taken the time to pause and view the natural complexity we have all been gifted.*

It was a taxing night for Mara. She locked eyes with the ceiling for hours before forcing herself to sleep. Even then, her slumber was a greeting for nightmares...

She stood before the judges. Her hands were chained together as though she were a criminal ravenous for illegal activity. The skin of her forearms burned. A child's loud cries detained her ears. She was suffocating in the tight grip of another's palms. The wooden seats of the jury scraped against the floor to mask the child's yelling. The banging of the gavel reverberated within the room. Mara felt as though she were underwater; every sound was heard, but distantly. An echo into the unknown. Shouts severed her throat as three officers dragged her away from the courtroom. Mara kept pulling, shaking, and screaming to set herself free, until she woke up.

Her eyes evaded the taunting bathroom light. Beside her, on the nightstand, was Camber's journal. She was tempted to read it, hoping it would calm her nerves. It would only be for a moment. Handwritten in black ink...

Life is not something I choose to mess with. In the worst of times, it beheads me with the ultimate punishment. Her smile radiates dopamine that courses throughout each atom I breathe in. Something about her, the miles of oceans that drag along in her mind. Something that holds her back and forces her to look away from me. I love her so very, very much…and she does not know it. She will not know it. I picture nights of lying beside such a frail angel. Caring for her when no one else will. Fighting her demons as though they are my own. Working years of labor to provide her with everything she ever dreamed of.

Could she care for me as much as I care for her? Is it possible to love someone so much without them ever noticing? Or is it a rotten obsession? In my mind, I dream only of her. When I think of her, I do not just think. My mind truly wanders into the depths of possibility.

Could this text be speaking of me? Camber had paragraphs written about a girl he loved so deeply. Mara was not entirely sure who it was, but she continued to read the truths scribbled in his handwriting.

Maybe I was once accustomed to the usual flow of a natural life. One where the only longings were those for ice-cream past midnight or a new toy. A life so immaculate. Where fear came from tales of knights and midnight creatures. I understood nothing but learned I had to take something on eventually. A journey. One where I could become whomever I wanted to be. 'An astronaut, a teacher,' they used to say. 'A lawyer!' Funny. Now, years later, I wish I were a lawyer. Prove to her I had become someone great, so that she would love me even more.

After experiencing the act of obsessing over someone, I can never not be obsessed with her. Sprouting from me are weeds that entangle her and bring her closer; yet, she believes they are petals from roses and clouds of white. How naive I believe she is. To allow such a lying stranger into her life. Yet something is different; wrong seems right, and right seems wrong. Her laughter resonates as much as her striking appearance. Darkened moons can turn bright with the veracity she exudes. She entertains me; for a reason I cannot decipher. Maybe it is her beauty or the personality that inhibits her soul and differs from others. The hours fly by as the minutes lie still, and I continue to disguise the worst parts of myself. Deep down, I know there is something wrong. She has her own sorrows from her past. She leans in closer, as I begin to fall for her. I cannot, and I should not. If I do, it would not be right. My desire could bring pain to both her and me. Her comfort with me is frightening. However, in the moment, I urge my cravings away since my soul knows that I am addicted to her. What a wondrous and extraordinary girl who can regress my abysmal thoughts.

From the start, I knew that she would be the one who would create this everlasting sense of joy in my heart. I don't know what we are, neither does she. But as long as we're together, everything is clear. I love her. That, I cannot deny. We care for each other in ways I didn't know were possible. A desire to make her happy has appeared, and no one can change my mind. Such a fragile creature, but adorable, she is. This girl is mine to protect and discover.

Oh, how bright the days have passed. Unlike others, I love her. She comforts the deadly desires in me into something beautiful. No words can bring me such happiness. Maybe it is pure temptation, maybe it is something more, but inside of me grows a passion that I cannot control. Who could soften a demonic soul with a look of the eye? Honestly, it is true when I say, a look of the eye has a deeper meaning than a conversation in vigorous sea. However, with her, either of those is worth more than a million jewels. Her value is infinite. Countless nights I spend with her. She will never be aware of the impact she creates on my own fragile interior. I was once frozen until she saved me from myself. I have melted. I am forever grateful for the warmth she brings to me.

Text seemed to be scribbled out, but overall his writing matched the delusion which Mara enjoyed reading in books.

The moonlight dimmed, allowing nightly comfort for those selfish enough to drift to sleep. Thoughts roamed in Mara's mind, overcoming her consciousness until stars became random shapes of light floating behind her closed eyelids. Life was so much more fulfilling when consciousness ceased. False reality gave the gift of escape, making it possible to find another world. In a way, she was now able to relate more to Camber. They were both outcasts and had suffered from two versions of loneliness.

Morning came. Camber, on the chair, questioned Mara on her perception of love; whether it was a beautiful blessing or the vulnerability involved would end up hurting someone. He recited a poem that pertained to the question.

"Laughter.

That's the audio that plays in the montage.

It's your laughter.

Leading the images of our twisted romance.

It's your smile that I pause on.

Gives me a dose of serotonin.

You can't replicate that smile.

I'll tell you why.

When it's real.

Your eyes soften.

The way you look at me.

I don't think you've looked at anyone like that.

I know it.

Because when you smile I feel like I've discovered
      what no one's come across.

I love the montage.

But somehow as soon as I press play.

I don't enjoy it anymore.

When it starts to show I can only think of how it is
      going to end.

That it is finite.

Our story.

I count seconds down instead of watching the pictures.

When I see your smile, I pause.

And I drag to the next clip.

Because seeing your smile end is like seeing the sun set for the last time.

I close my eyes before the last few seconds.

So the end of us doesn't seem real.

Maybe the next season hasn't come out yet.

But the months go on.

And I still haven't heard of their renewal.

So if anyone can please let me know.

I'd appreciate it."

The addiction is so blinding that I cannot imagine what the absence of the other person would do to someone. When vision is restored and mind cleared, would there not be a gaping hole in one's heart? What if the other person takes advantage of your affection?

Camber and Mara both craved the positive, better

side that lacked in the world's population. What forced the masses around them to feel entitled to hurt and destroy? Camber was just like Mara. Lost on a path steered by emotions, blinded by colors of shadowed translucence. *I guess we look around and hope that negativity isn't the only thing the world has and maybe, maybe people aren't as broken as we are.*

If there is one common pain I know not of, it is love. The beauty and beast of the world. Imagery designs its course through petals of roses, tulips, violets, and colors of brightened futures, but then death plummets down a cliff to rocks and crashing waves. Whispers of Camber's deep voice released Mara from fiction. Then he fell silent, wondering what could possibly be going on in a mind such as Mara's.

It is impossible to understand everything that flies into the mind of another. But I know. His eyes moved quietly, but the slight ruffling of his hair triggered her.

He finally spoke again. "Have you ever pictured the pains of the world all at once? When your imagination swears of all horrid things? How humans have access to the souls of others, entrapping them in their own minds? When those of higher power hold keys to their physical corpses? When one's happiness is chained with the locks of another?"

CHAPTER 10

Perhaps it was the change of environment and new experiences that allowed Mara to forget her origins for a moment. Maybe there was such a thing as someone who could resonate with her.

I've always questioned how individuals could have such differences in morality. Well, what is humanity? Masses of people inhabiting the Earth with their various ideas, but what of them? While it may seem we must judge the ideas of others when they do not align with our own, why don't we take the time to understand what led them to believe in them? The reader of every book—of every piece of information that has been inscribed, thought, or felt—has experienced someone else's emotions. Some of these emotions are seen as unacceptable, unwanted. You aren't allowed to feel anything until it fits the other's definition of what deserves to be felt.

I've been through moments where this separation from others' compassion has been impossible to handle. Mankind is meant to be tested, but the level of difficulty also depends on how much an individual can withstand. That's what I like to tell myself. How much willpower do they have? What do they have to live for? How much do they want it? It's no matter of quality or quantity. It's a continuous cycle. Would they continue through the process of this demanding journey for those they feel they have a responsibility to? Deep down inside, that feeling should not be viewed as a negative. The impossible that clouds every living soul is actually what creates hope, it's when you don't know what will happen or the chance that it might not. For I would live to finally see this supposed beauty. Not for the pointless, nonpermanent desires that I know are meant to obstruct my judgment from the flowers that are taking their time to blossom. I will admit the quick distractions do tempt me more each time the highs subside. They grow. They grow.

However! Life does not do as you expect or hope. I cannot prevent my own story from happening by hiding behind literature. I believe literature to be the only way to be understood without having to address another. It is a great way to relate to others. Nevertheless, I cannot live in fiction. I must live and experience in the moment of reality.

Mara and Camber drove through hills that dissolved into mist. She wondered where their destination would be. Camber had led her inside the car keeping her clueless. The breeze entered through his open window and exited through hers. Every now and then, another car drove by, but otherwise, they traveled along the road in solitude. *It is nice to have someone sitting beside you. Someone with whom to share the experience. Companionship.*

Mara had fallen asleep; however, a tight feeling in her chest awoke her. When her eyes refocused, she discovered a petrifying view beyond the car's windshield. Petrifying due to its familiar doom. She knew exactly where they were.

Camber looked at her. "We must face the things that hold us back. Shadows from your past that prevent you from growing must be shone upon. You need to force yourself through the walls. And once you break them with your fist, you must let the walls and your fist bleed. When you try to push something away, it will linger until you address it. Overcome it. The longer you ignore, the more hold it will have over you. It needs to be confronted, or else it might start showing up when you really don't want it to. Don't let it get to that point, Mara. Remember, it is so important to revisit the broken foundations in your life in order to heal. You should do this, for yourself and for your future."

CHAPTER 11

Little rocks scattered into the air, and dust cascaded across the windshield. Below, the tires ran over shards of beer bottles. The radio had been turned off, allowing the engine to take over. Camber drove through the town's entrance, passing Mr. Bartholomew's cafe and the homes of uneasy farmers and depressed alcoholics. *I wonder where their sadness stems from. Perhaps it breeds from knowledge; when there is awareness there can be more, but there is failure in reaching it. Knowledge may seem attractive when looking at people who have a larger hold on it; however, the amount of accompanied suffering deters its value. Painful.*

Tears formed in the corners of Mara's eyes. Returning reminded her of the feeling of entrapment. It seemed as though years of her life had been taken from her here. She had been wilting away, never having had the opportunity to escape. *Just like Father. But I found freedom, finally. It kills me to know that someone out there could be awaiting a second chance at life, hoping to be shown the world, but it never happens. People here are born to prepare for their death. In a sense, to look forward to their death. Waiting to pass away as though life had not existed at all. Death in exchange for the glimpse of life. Blackmail.*

Mara opened the window, and her tangled hair flew in every direction. One by one, locals extended their necks to inspect the foreign vehicle. Mara slumped in her seat, petrified of the rest of the drive but incapable of pressing the brakes.

Children here could not even turn to their parents for guidance. They were clueless. Information they retained was the remnants of what their own parents had passed down to them. *Adults and children are unable to offer each other anything but the monotonous lifestyle they find themselves surrounded by.* Perishing in the center of Mara's chest, her heart pumped out its sorrowful tears and a sense of danger infused her blood; years of abuse would never escape the depths of her core. *The basis of my life is composed by the horrid years of my upbringing. But people who use the past as an excuse will never attain the life they wish.*

Camber followed the path to her child home as if he already knew it. He understood Mara in ways others could never. Why would she ever relinquish such a unique connection? It came upon Mara—as things would—that darkness would soon disguise the day. Her mother was not as welcoming as one wished a mother to be, and word of Mara's presence would run quickly throughout Ranches, causing turmoil. No one ever left the town. Or ever came. So the pair decided to spend the night under the stars, and Mara would have to face her mother the following day. Eternal disruption seemed meek compared to the idea of coming face-to-face with her mother. But Mara had no choice, for Mother was all that remained to haunt her.

Camber parked the car in a deserted bit of land. Once they stepped outside, the world was silent. Deep inside Mara's chest, the clicking of locks echoed. Camber spread blankets on the grass, and they reclined together. Within a few minutes, he fell into a deep sleep. Mara's eyes remained open, afraid of time's effect. She needed to confront her mother, now. Would she make it back before Camber woke up? No doubt ran through her mind. She was off.

CHAPTER 12

It was past two-thirty in the morning. A dominating clocktower built of cheap, red brick, established its authority over the town. The crimson popped among the beige storefronts below. Trembling along the sidewalk was Mara, a veil swaddled around her head. She raged with emotion. *It is difficult to find closure with something that has no end. However, once truly felt, a conclusion is beyond rewarding.*

Mara spotted Mr. Bartholomew's rusting cafe, and she ran past it. Then, she saw the dark aura of her childhood home. Her father's beat up car was still parked out front. She looked at her room's window. It was partially open, and the lights were on. Extremely dim, but on. Mara dug her fingernails into her palms, numbing the other pain she felt within.

Perhaps Camber was the fuel to Mara's newfound flames. He motivated her to accomplish the things she never would. Had it not been for him, she would be destroyed. *There is no feeling worse than loneliness. Maintaining the comfort of status quo rather than taking a risk for change leads to self-destruction; the fear of growth destroys individuals.*

From seed births tree, flower, fruit; until, human characteristics unfold to the fruitlet, dividing the skin from within. Flies scatter and swarm around the remnants of rotten flesh.

It began to rain, so Mara rushed to the window before she would drown. *A surplus of emotion can cause a person to forget about the effects it has on others. It also destroys. Yet that person may eventually apologize, and life goes on. A vicious cycle once again.*

It would be much easier for me to never confront my mother, to live in the fictional land of what could have been rather than have a definite answer. Nevertheless, I must make the effort to speak with her in order to tie the loose ends in yet another chapter of my life. Others may excel to another page of their book without having to endure the difficult emotions tied to the current one, but I cannot. What happens after my interaction with her will cease to be in my control. It is not as important.

The wet wind blew against Mara's cheeks, calming the flush. She peeked further into the window. In the corner of the room sat a woman, a familiar woman. The raindrops sounded like warning alarms. But Mara did not pull back.

CHAPTER 13

Gloom rose over Mara as her eyes faltered. The hall leading to the room she was in could be seen through the door left ajar. Mara could taste a hint of lime in the air. Somehow, her body craved the bewitching fragrance more than she had ever dreamt. As her vision sharpened, four emerald walls entrapped her further. Mara's mind receded into the timeline of what had led up to her current setting. She had fallen from the height of the window. Her mother must have heard the thud of her body and taken her inside.

Mara's lips tasted of blood and consciousness grew through her corpse, reaching her fingertips. They were trembling. Lime… Mara desperately wanted to inhale more of it, to bathe in its appealing high.

Imagine that weak female; the one tied to the tracks of a train. What if patriarchy overwhelmed her to the extent of uselessness? She is internally coerced to believe the only way to see a better world is at night when she is able to dream of it. Dreamers. Love, egalitarian societies, powerful impossibilities are viewed as general goals, but why? Has anyone attempted to truly understand? To listen to the cries of the silenced? Man only perceives life through a quadrant. What goes on around depends on distance; the farther away, the less it is understood. Privilege relies not on monetary value, but on the upbringing and care one receives. I wish I was taught value in my life. The value of caring for my health, my mind, and my emotions. I live, I long for nothing, and I rot slowly to my demise.

Mara's limbs threatened to detach themselves from her core, so that she could run freely. Yet fear overwhelmed her. It was not what had brought the fear, but rather, what was still left to overcome. It was the bleak emerald walls of the room that scared her. The years of pain she endured were infused in the paint, the ceiling, and the furniture. Mara could not run or shout. Would she ever be able to escape the chokehold this place had on her?

Mara heard her mother's steps. All she could do was lay there listening. And then she appeared, wearing a filthy flannel sweater. Eyes half awake, but still whole if possible.

Chain me. Torture me. But let her not see. I cannot blind her myself, I can never do that to her. She still lives within me. Her distant memory will never fade. My childhood innocence keeps me somewhat intact, and I am nonetheless hurt. I have never once been able to choose the things that hurt me.

"Come on," the woman said.

Mara finally built the courage to stand up and walk alongside Mother. With each step, she was thrust further inside the body she inhabited to protect her. Together, they traveled through the hallway.

CHAPTER 14

Steered by all things mad, the woman dusted the kitchen countertop with her calloused palms and took a seat. Her voice filled the air, crackling as she dragged her words. "Indentured," Mother said. "The only fit trait to describe your purpose. The only reason you inhabit this Earth so freely. As much as you try to escape this natural hold that is on you, you cannot. Your efforts will continue to fail. That's why I am here, Mara. You have always had these fantasies in your head that guide you through life blindly. Trust me, we are the same. This control over your life that you seek does not exist. You are a woman. Your desire for freedom clashes with deep rooted ideas of femininity. Look at me. Our sex determines our destiny. Your mentality remains intertwined with it as does your cowardly attempt to divert from it. You cannot run. Your mind is a useless piece gifted to you by your own kind. And you serve the same purpose with or without it. Weak. I watched you destroy everything before you even began. An unfortunate soul determined to push through the bounds of immortality only to find another wall. You know, Mara, we are similar in many ways. We were put into this life without consent. You have been led astray, and now I will guide you back to reality."

Emotions aren't meant to be steady, they fluctuate. And this inconsistency? It will always inhibit one's stability. We test ourselves. In multiple ways. Plath through the courage of death. Astaire through the risk of redundancy and failure. Andromache with the invincibility of fate. Madness gently takes over, like a disease, blurring the lines between reality and fiction until the brain rots. Joy is a bipolar feeling, nonpermanent, but forever craved. And mankind craves what it cannot have. So joy continues to be searched for. Joy relinquishes a trail of mixed stratagems, for it doesn't wish to be found. There are things that resemble joy, take on its role in disguise; fooling not only the gullible, but the wisest. For joy is something so craved that people begin to imitate it. So life dwindles and people continue searching for a way out of its misery.

There is an unfortunate grin in the eyes of a merciless conqueror who touches the feeble skin of a powerless victim. The world revolves in shallow inferiority as they gloat in victorious heights. All else fails, all else but supremacy. But here, a victim decides to become a predator.

"I'm nothing like you. I didn't have the privilege of having a parent who was willing to sacrifice some of themself for me, to tell me what is right and wrong; which you are clearly unable to differentiate. How can a mother degrade her own daughter so willingly? I spent years trying to understand the reasons behind the way you treated me. Was I some evil virus you were afraid of? Now, I finally realize that whatever your reasons, they are not my cross to bear. "

Mother seemed unaffected. No, she was unaffected.

"I wanted to see you. I wanted my mother. I had to beg for your love. Plead for you to show me the slightest glimpse of humanity. You've always looked at me with such despair. Why have me to begin with? Why bring me into a life of suffering? This feeling of resentment I have toward you is unlike any other." Dying into the edges of the world, the sun made its final appearance. "But we are not the same. As much as I hate you, I care for you equally, and I feel a massive amount of guilt for leaving. But, Mother, I cannot continue my life here. If this is our final interaction, understand there was never any ill intention behind my actions."

Mother stood before her daughter. She softened a little. For once, Mara felt the woman was processing as much as she had the ability to; her health had gotten worse since the last time she saw her. She was fading.

"You're leaving again?" Mother whispered.

"I am. Please do not try to stop me. I have seen a glimmer of happiness, and I must go after it."

They stood there in silence for what felt like forever. Mara knew it was time and made her way to the door. Mother stayed still. *I wish I could change her, but it is almost impossible to change the mentality of a grown person.*

"Bye, Mother. Be happy too." Mara left. All she could think of now was Camber. Where could he be? He must have woken up and realized she was not beside him. Mara pressed her soles into the soil and turned around. Coming from around the place she once called home, were two ears pointed upward and the outline of her best friend returning her gaze. She stood for a moment, her eyes locked with Hemingway's. Unable to process her emotions, she sprinted in the opposite direction. She ran in hopes of finding Camber. Maybe it was possible to remove humanity's injustices. An hour later, the clocktower rang. It never missed its cue. *It makes me think about a concept I easily relate to. When those oppressed are offered a chance to speak, they never miss it. Because they realize the value of being heard. It's nice to speak thoughts aloud. I'm used to expressing myself through literature and journaling. Maybe I should speak to others more often.*

Camber was exactly where Mara had left him. He was where she found her joy.

CHAPTER 15

Mara approached the plot of grass to a sleeping Camber. It was only a few hours ago that she had fled to speak with Mother, and yet it felt like ages since she had last seen him. She gazed at her lover, sound asleep, unconscious on the brink of dawn. *It scares me how easily it is for someone to die. Watching someone asleep reminds me of the last time I saw my father. His body horizontal, eyes shut just like Camber's. How sensitive our bodies are. How gentle a touch can be yet still be able to kill.*

Just as she stood over him, Camber awoke, blinking twice then meeting her eyes. Nautical blues fixed on the deep brown of hers. She could tell of his discomfort. They were both somewhere far from here. He, caught up in the sudden changes of his new life, trying to make sense of his feelings toward Mara. *As much as I want to live in the moment with him and only him, my mind cannot help but linger on my most recent interaction. Mother is dying. I could see it in the depth of her eyes, and as much as I hold her accountable for many negatives in my life, it was heartbreaking to see her so lost.*

Mara climbed over and curled on top of Camber. Her head shifted into his cozy shoulder. She was unable to focus. Mother's image infiltrating her mind caused anxiety to pile up. She could not help but still hold anger. Yes, Mara had said all that she needed to, but for the longest time, she believed her childhood was a mere normality. That love could only be found in her books. Mara wanted to find real love. An emotion she thought could stop the numbness and bring her back to life.

Camber grabbed her palm and said, "Mara, let's move on. Just you and I. We need to do this for us. Our future. Perhaps only a glimpse in time… But, honestly, life is but a timed test. It is easy to sulk and get caught up in grief, but if we want to accomplish anything, we need to put our thorough hearts to the task. It's the beautiful moments that build us and our stories. A novel, composed of all our mind's wonders. Let us fill it together. I want to experience life to the fullest with a partner. But only, and only when you have put your past aside. I see you hurt, each day, disintegrating into nothingness. But I know! I know! Her—your birth mother—that makes you feel as such. As though you rely on her to guide you. Not her, but what she has taught you…her effect. There is no past nor future, just present. So become my present, let it override the past and build the future. Override the past, Mara. Walk through the door that frightens you and return to me whole. I'm ready to love you completely."

Am I prepared to commit to an everlasting bond? Mara could not lose him, that she knew. Camber had become an important part of herself, the freedom to her wind; therefore, her attachment to him would result in a haunting loss if she were to deny him.

So Mara agreed. Fog engulfed the parked car. *Putting your will to live in the hands of another will fail you, but it eases the pain of living alone with your burdens.* Mara's grave, decorated by rotting vegetation, designed by the Earth's supremacy, was one yet to be uncovered by Camber. *Let him dig, and let him be blind. Let him cry not for me, but for the shadow I live in. Die in.*

"Camber, before we leave, I must visit someone else, alone. Give me a few hours, and I will meet you back here." Mara walked away from their campsite, deeper into the south of Ranches. Children of ten years and younger passed by, hats in their palms, wearing collared shirts and mangled socks. What shocked her was the truth in their grins, as though what they lived by became their happiness. *And that is what happens. When you know nothing else, you cannot compare your lifestyle to anything better or worse.*

She reached the cemetery and sat on the soil beside his headstone. Her father's name was plastered on it, mockingly yet nostalgically. She saw his hand reach out to her through the stone. She pulled on the hand. *Come back,* Father, *don't leave me any more than I wish to leave myself. I miss you. I don't care what you have done to me. I don't care what you let her do to me. My all is not here, you have taken part of it the day you died. Bring it back, please. Let's go, stop with the incessant game you play. My heart has withered almost completely. I don't feel anything but the pain of loss. Numb to everything. A child, I am still, Father.* Their hands intertwined. Mara glared at the frigid fingers she held so tightly. *I'm—I'm so sorry.* She shook her head and the hand disappeared. *I would rather it be me to suffer anyway.*

Thunder destroyed the insides of her ears, so she closed the holes with the tips of her index fingers, creating a wall between reality and fiction. She closed her eyes.

A young Mara tiptoed into Father's room, smiling and looking upward to meet her parents' eyes. But her mother forced her out. Her jejune toes retreated across the wooden floor, right back to her room. She lay beside the door, caressing its disfigured face. "I love you. You want to know something, door? I appreciate you. Mr. Leroy from my new novel says you need to tell people that. Or else they feel useless. Humans don't really like each other. But it's okay, because I like them. I will love everything so that no one else has to. Don't worry, door, I love you. Sweet dreams, see you tomorrow." Under her mattress, Mara revealed two dolls. Mother and Father. Even if they did not want her there, she wanted them here. "Goodnight. I love you too."

She opened her eyes and once again, she was face-to-face with her father's name. She stared at it for a bit longer then compelled her legs to walk away. A difficult task. *It is not the details that linger into present time that hold power over us, it is the effects of a single event from the past that impact us most. The instances one wishes to forget but that have already done their damage.*

Mara returned to Camber. Retracing her steps, seeing the children once more. Their honorable grins. *The broken child within Mara has awoken. She is running. She runs with the wind. Pushing toward eternity.*

I know deep inside, she is not the issue. She continues to drag forward into the unknown. But I? No. I am immobile, knees breaking inward to cope with the lustrous weight. When one tries to run, the other breaks. Two poles. Yet opposites attract. One cannot live with a mirror image of itself. People often prove themselves only by curtaining their mirror-images. Pushing toward recognition rather than acceptance. But the past version of myself and the current? We view other sides of the world. Hiding from change through pain.

And Mara returned to Camber, as selfish as she was, to chase him around in the hopes of escaping her past. How long had it been? She could not tell. But she was back. Back to the car by the grasses and the harsh breeze that abused those grasses. Back next to Camber, never again to be separated. Mara was back home.

PART TWO

CHAPTER 16

Behind the cartridges of ink there lay a plume, and beside that plume a small sprouting plant barely held its leaves by the stem, drooping so low as if pleading for fertile soil. *For when something is alone, any item of any kind will appeal to it.* The objects created a hazy silhouette against the desk upon which they were propped. In the center, a pensioned journal seemed touched only moments ago.

The home was silent, and the objects were sitting still as they always were. But the clock on the wall adjacent to them continued to tick. Once every second and sixty times every minute. The mice in the cabinets had only just started to show, and the lights were off. A woman walked in bearing a child, a father followed a few ticks after. Moaning in his exhausted mother's bosom, the baby was wrapped in a silky blue sheath, face so smooth like clay just beginning to set. The father lovingly patted the woman's head.

After placing the life in its new bassinet, Mara overlooked the clock and glanced at her husband. Matted around her ring finger was a crafted piece of metal from the nearest forge, the color of copper. She seemed pleased enough. When he requited her gaze, there held a hidden connection. And a lack of one.

"Time has traveled through our own selves, perhaps bringing back our destined fates from one wormhole into another. Two separate spaces that we each fail to acknowledge. Damian links them together. Camber, would you like to spend the night beside him? I can bring in the bed covers from the masterpiece."

Camber looked into the bassinet. His face shone in the most prudent way. All else was meaningless when compared to his and his son's presence. A spark between them ignited instantly. Camber returned to his own childhood. Ignorant. Nothing could take his mind away from focusing on his child, and no act was to be expressive enough nor out of bounds. Damian's facial features favored his father's. Deep within, both parents were afraid of the child's upbringing. Two undefined pasts were to blend into an unstable medley, and none could prevent it nor understand it. Ever. The parents, therefore, focused on how they would influence the child's innocence from habit and evil.

Placing his palm onto the child's forehead, Camber muted all else and felt the warmth. Mara stood by. "He is calm," she said. "Let us get the covers and pillows. He is alright. Allow him to adapt to this foreign environment."

"You created such a wonderful home for the young soul these last few months. But yes, he will adapt."

"Do you mind putting him to bed? I'm going to take a bath."

Agreeing to her request, the new father made haste and retrieved the bedding. Mara prepared for bed. As usual, she rotated the bath knob to the warmest temperature, submerged her frail physique, and reclined to gaze at the ligneous room. Reaching for the ancient flask of lime-scented soap, she accidentally knocked it over. *An artifact. How captivating! How can an item so worn out earn an even greater value? Imagine if people were to work in that same way. Where the foulest trait we perceive of ourselves is the one most loved by others. Where our price is based on the priceless quality of our worst genes. Maybe then, we would not drain our lives in search of ridding ourselves of the things that make us who we are. Alas, people do not live as such, and to dream these dreams is only to escape momentarily from the lack of bliss in reality. What do we live for? If it is not for myself, then I see no value.*

Even the birth of Mara's newborn did not appeal to her. And Camber... Bless his heart. She cared no more for him than the dying leaves of a tree in the fall. She approached each season in the dark, and when winter hit she would watch as the snow numbed her and withered her corpse even more.

Perhaps it was wrong to say she did not feel for the child nor her husband, but Mara thought the truth and it only. *I am watching my story unfold in black and white, unbothered by its lack of colors and emotions. Whatever might bring life to the world, mine is platonic.*

So each night, Mara bathed and prepared for the end, but she was stuck in a loophole. Each morning, she awoke again to the usual blinding sun. She could not drown. And for such a beacon of cleansing, the dear sun lived to tempt her, distracting her mind from doubt. Yet she was so certain of her pain. Not a natural one, but one that birthed from desolation. *Why can't I feel? What demons must chain me from my humanity? I do not know emotions, I live by none. I lie here still, and I speak here still. But no sustenance keeps me alive. Nor attempts to. I am already dead.*

Look at the people in my past, Father. Look at how they eye me. Did you place them? Did you place them to taunt me? To mock my trust? I am tormented by your luminance. And no lust have I demonstrated. No envy have I presented. My cries drip underneath the throne of your lap.

Mara lay still in the bath. The water surged, submerging her world into the depths of another hell. Surpassing the gates with such confidence, only to witness pools of eternally flowing blood, skeletons of undead children fighting to keep their heads above water. Wailing for their abandoned parents. *Even the worst turn to their innocence when their freedom is taken away. Perhaps when God is not available, it is those who have already arrived who hold the most wisdom. Hope is what pursues their eternal damnation; however, it is also the largest piece to play in terms of pain. An ace.*

It was quiet. So quiet. *It is almost pleasing to know that silence does not inhibit repose. One learns to drift away.* But as Mara perched on the grounds of perdition, numbness called her into the pits of the wise lands. And it almost felt real. The whirlpool strengthened, and Mara was suspended into absolute zero. She latched onto her forearms, freezing from the cold. Then she realized they weren't quiet. She was quiet. She was drowning.

"Mara! How much longer are you going to take? Mara! Where is the pacifier? Each time I try to fall asleep, he wakes me!" Camber yelled.

Mara unfastened the latches to her eyelids. *I know now where I am eventually destined. The Devil has already shown me his realm.*

It's not his fault she could not be what he needed. Mara's own avarice inundated her desire to continue to serve in the fantasy family. She crumbled on her own; therefore, instead of burdening them with her troubles, she would fight them herself. Alone. As always.

"Honey, it is beneath the towel we brought only hours ago." Mara glanced at the clock, reminding her of the passing time. Eleven thirty-nine. Wrapped around her core, pressed against her chest, was a towel, suffocating any feeling of a future. "Don't forget to warm the child's sustenance before you fall asleep, dear. I'll check on him in the morning before I leave."

Mara worked as a maid in the day and took on the responsibility of watching over the family's child, Agnes. She cared for the other child as if she were her own. Only six years younger than she, yet there was little difference. She kept to herself, reading in her room. When Mara peeked into her dormitory—which was always left open— Agnes would look momentarily, only to smile and signal a welcome into the room. Fifteen years of age; nevertheless, barely an infant. The child was well-versed in biblical terminology and all the classic literature in the world. Unfortunately, it was apparent her mother and father lacked the time to care for her, and so, she lacked the love that both she and Mara dreamt of.

No lover can gift such a thing, and no drug can numb the lifelong pain that continues to eat at you...slowly. Unnoticeable, most of the time, but so clear to the empathizer. They know the truth, the misery. And you run around hurting others, breaking them down—to their lowest —while you thrive in their demise. Until their hurt resembles yours. You blind yourself with others in order to stop having to face your demons alone. Distractions on distractions. Misery loves company. Loneliness, unlike solitude, brings the temptations that ruin life. Our lives. Infamous for inflicting pain on others while unable to heal our own. Hypocrisy. But it does feel better than living alone.

So she and I? We live as strangers, outcasts for the world to blindside. They won't ever understand. Oblivious to the devil that lives within us. It cries of banishment into a state of fear where nothing is left to turn to. And what makes it so demonic is the force of nothingness that lives there. Nothing and pain are synonymous, and their repetitive natures allow them to flourish. It is so cold. So cold. That's what numbs everything. Yet we continue to search for anything to make us feel. Anything. And when we are fortunate enough to feel, we don't wish to feel alone.

CHAPTER 17

"Mara, could you come over? I want to share this challenging piece with you, but I can't fully explain it myself. Maybe you are able to? It's as though it is meant to have been personally felt, and yet I cannot find any sentiment nor warmth with it."

Mara was watching over Agnes today. The two shared great commonalities, one of which was a fondness for poetry. "I'm coming, Agnes. Show me."

A soul born from a faded tear
One who flourished not but hid

The colors were lost before the first sight of air

Breath and life

But time comes someone enters

For the first time not pushed away

A perfect spirit that removed all fear

Thrust the ghosts that grasped onto the water

Brought love three words

But fear walked along the tightrope leading to nerves

Afraid of being replaced

The tear enhanced itself

Grew envy worse than previous pain

Enveloped itself with possessiveness and greed

And over time

The one who brought light had fled

The candle in the twilight had deserted

And darkness roamed the mind of the soul

Agony returned twenty times worse

A devil had grown

But the fire had burned out.

"You won't leave, will you, Mara? I feel as though we understand each other. Nobody truly understands me." Agnes looked down.

Mara was on the verge of promising commitment,

when truly, she knew she had no capability of keeping such a thing. "You know, Agnes, you should never feel ashamed of such a truth. I look at the clouds sometimes, wanting to blend with the atmosphere, begging the wind to drag me with it." *I will do what you ask of me, just stay with me. And chain me so I don't leave you. I know...Aeolus, I know I will run from you. But do not let me! I am so lonely. Turn me into dust and shut my mind. Anything it takes to make you stay. Just let me know you are with me.* "The world will agonize you at times, I must warn. There is not a single thing you can do to prevent it, unfortunately. When spoken of, they will criticize you, judge you—although, at first, they will beg you to share your thoughts. 'It's healthy, it's normal,' they will say. And, the first few times, your desire to melt and release all that holds you will exceed your experience, it's okay. But, over time, it becomes engraved in their reactions that they care no less, for they all have their personal issues."

"I hate that, Mara. I'm so vulnerable. It's as though I trapped myself and I can't escape. My silly mind has forgotten the code and will never remember it."

Mara sat beside her, but what more could she say? Deny her statement? Tell her it was not true? Tell her of the world's beauties? Which beauties? The men that live to torment women of their chastity? The voices of hypocrisy that all live to supersede? No, no, to keep her mouth closed from useless words seemed much more efficient. It was better she learned herself than be told and scared by another. "Agnes, let's leave the house for a little. Your parents return in a few hours. It is clear you spend your time paranoid and overthinking, let's take a walk. We can bring the cat along, is that alright?"

Reluctantly, the girl nodded in agreement.

Beacon of misery, won't you come down? I can't fathom the choices I have made. To me, it all seems hazy. But when light obliges and darkness compels, it becomes clear. Sitting on the grass and balling her eyes is my past self in front of her dismal Hemingway. And I gaze at the monstrosity. For it is not myself there upon the sheet of green, but the soul from which I bled from. Him, ingesting the vegetation, and I, blanketing myself with its frail comfort.

They strolled the neighborhood, both quiet and focused on the path. Mara turned to face Agnes, and the world around her darkened. Her eyes were struggling to remain open, and her limbs laid frail beside her. "Agnes?" The girl stood motionless. "Agnes!" There was that familiar scent of lime that began to flow. The scent became stronger, and she could not escape it as it clogged her mind, until she remembered. She remembered the fragrance, and she spun back and forth until Agnes returned to the real Agnes. And Hemingway was still in the town of Ranches, eating away at the end of his life.

"Mara! Mara! Are you alright?!" Agnes rushed toward her maid and latched onto her. "Put it down, Mara! I beg you! Let it go."

What could she possibly be referring to? Mara looked at her own two palms, carved with lines of fortune. In the right, she held a pocket knife. Further below, there was a cut on her knee. "Agnes, what has happened? What have you done, child?"

"What have I done, Mara?" The girl stuttered in fear. "We were walking before you started to attack me. You slit your knee as you swung the knife. Then you turned to me!"

"And how have I managed to find myself on the grass then? You are speaking lies, Agnes. Where would I find this knife? It is not mine. Why would I do such a thing?" *How enervating this girl!* "Let's go back to the house. Never to speak of this again. I will not inform your parents; be thankful for my patience." *I attacked her? What nonsense!*

People enjoy taking things away from others, regardless of what the good may say. No one is good; it's a loose term. And my heart breaks each time, I swear, no wonder why I struggle so much. I have felt before...but nothing new. I have felt every torch of terror. And, yet, men flourish with their brethren's downfall.

CHAPTER 18

Mara, at fifteen years old, had been pressured by the minute to become someone she wished not to, and yet, the sole thing that kept her sane was useless to another. Her Hemingway. *As most people in life will come to terms with, there is always something stronger than life's most miserable whirlwind. The same instinct that lovers fight for in their half. Attachment fragments the bonds that tie us to our toxicity. And in times of brutality, it brings us to our knees in order to be able to return to something stable and consistent in our lives. But in order for another's pleasure to be fulfilled, it requires one's own demise. You cannot truly appreciate happiness unless you have experienced what it means to be sad and miserable.* So Mara grew with the goat. And to escape the confinement of her stagnant life, she had to tear herself from the one she would die for... And so she did. Something else within her died that day. For when she went outside, the weather stormed, but the thunder did not instill fear, and the lightning did not compel her to blink. She drowned in the paradise of flooding. *How ironic it is. I had to take care of myself to make sure he was cared for, yet his absence released me from needing to prioritize my well-being. Why care for myself anymore? Let alone anyone?*

"Miss! Would you be able to hand me a glass of water and some food? I'm starving!" Agnes cried from her bedroom.

Out of the ordinary, is it not? For someone usually so quiet to take advantage of me now, after all this time. The family's house was rather small, with a kitchen and its seating, a bathroom shared by two cramped bedrooms, each with the ability to enter through the conjoined middle portion, and a quarter for the maid.

"Did you hear me?"

What a change in the child's tone! Should she continue to speak this way—

"Let's not forget what happened!"

And Mara prepared the oven. "Of course, child, whatever your will may be, place it upon me." Granulated sugar, dry yeast, salt, oil, flour, all combined and kneaded upon the kitchen counter. Her knuckles pressed into the mixture, stretching it apart further.

Agnes's parents were never home. Mara pitied her, wondering what it was like for a child to contemplate how their parents lived before their arrival, sometimes never realizing it was unplanned. That their souls were the result of a meaningless mistake. The batter stuck to Mara's fingernails. Not that she knew of when Damian was conceived, it never made sense, for it had been scarcely seven months when she gave birth. He had no congenital deformities, nor was his health in any way faltering. Mara twisted and turned the dough, stretching the edges and forcing them back in.

When one stood outside the family's house, the acacia bark presented a warm tone, and one could imagine a loving family inhabiting the walls within, digressing from the will of the world's unhappiness, poverty, and lack of self-restraint. *Unfortunately, with time, man's greatest failure is to see what is in front of them. Not directly underlined, but written in between.*

As Mara faced the window between the house's exterior disguise and its rotting interior, she caught a glimpse of Agnes's reflection. Eyes focused on her little fingers wrapped around the knife.

Sanity rekindled the torches of truth. But Mara still wondered what had happened; the pieces in her mind were much too blurred to be put together. Without any sort of confirmation, she assumed Agnes had disappeared into her room, so she returned to the sticky mixture and placed it in the oven.

Mara wondered what it would be like to live the rest of her life pursuing conventional family life. Was there more the world had to offer? She abandoned the comfort of Ranches in order to experience for herself the beautiful writings she read about in books. The color of the real world. The everlasting joy she was meant to feel after falling in love and starting her own family. Maybe there was a step in between she missed. Had she done it right, she would surely feel more fulfilled.

There is an emptiness within me that grows larger by the day. A sense of normality that saddens me. The world has become accustomed to me. God dedicated his energy to release me from my hometown, and now he has moved on to another that calls him. Adventure is gone. Is this what I will do forever? Tend to Agnes, Camber, and Damian?

That was it. Mara would leave in the morrow. Distance was all that called her. And she would journey on. Who would ever choose to sit and suffer in such constant dullness? A housemaid. A servant. A husband's woman. A child's mother. Mara wanted more from life.

CHAPTER 19

You know how the world speaks of the promises of the unknown? Fatality is the dream we wish to pursue, and this infernal Earth which we currently inhabit will seem a mere taste of our strength. That what does not kill you makes you stronger; however, I have always questioned it. Is that why knives tempt the orgasm of the soul? Is that why the psychotics of mankind cut themselves? Well, why should they be labeled as mentally ill because of their courage to admit their unhappiness in this world? No one is happy in this world, and those who exhibit it the most have suffered to the point where an alias is the simplest solution. And these people? We thank them. Because their ability to disguise their pain is accepted as more appropriate. It's true, we should thank them. I pursue my path of fate only to rush it until I can no longer run. And I know, as I look to the door that entices destiny, I can lose everything. Leaving means I will never be able to return, but I already know the outcome of my life if I am to stay.

Three streets led Mara onward, and to choose from either seemed burdening for when she stepped out into the intersection, she stood stuck between the lines. One street took her toward the congested, mainstream vehicles, bumper to bumper. In the second, lights flickered on and off, malfunctioning by the hands of mankind. The third street curved along the edges of natural flora. Three paths she had already taken, yet not one felt right. Therefore, Mara stood immobile at the intersection. Cars approached, and when the drivers dropped their windows to ask her the matter, she said, "How come you sit and ask me why I block your way, and yet two other paths are before you to choose from? Although I balance to and fro, I hold no grip to either, and no grip is there to hold me. If you wished to continue, you would raise your speed, pushing the limits of your car. Why stop and affect the moment of time? I stand here to watch you choose the path that entices you in the second, regardless of my presence."

And not one of them understood her. Not one cared after the first sentence. *Mankind turns blind when they are unable to comprehend. But why should they care, if not for the answer they wish to hear?* The drivers raised their window shut and chose the path of traffic. Was it a fear of leaving the crowd? Or were they following natural instinct?

So Mara pivoted to face the other end of the main road and resumed her departure. *Is it but I who realizes the imaginative perspective of life that is more fulfilling than the tangible reality? Our minds are capable of overcoming the objects directly in front of us. But they deceive us into praying and believing in something else.*

Tell me not one man has dreamed that the woman he loves will love him back. The silent stares. Withering at the blink of her eye, the smiles she recites. The aspiration to touch her skin, to hold her hand, only to brush against her arm for a moment. Therefore, would it not be easier to dream of a world where all is exactly how you wish it to be? Where the other loves you just as much? I can't understand how others blindly follow their routines with no desire or free will.

Why could Mara not flow with the fundamental

ideals of life itself? On this thrilling evening, the eyes of a sparrow locked on her as lavender pollen and pedals plummeted to the tips of her shoes. Perhaps along the paved road she would find her lost soul, somewhere between the flora and fauna. Perhaps this new beginning would finally satiate her curiosity. She was addicted to not knowing what came next. So much so that she removed herself from the secure life that was gifted to her.

As Mara continued along the pedways, reptiles and annelids danced around her feet. She took a seat at the next bus stop to play with them. Their sloppy epidermis whirled against her thumb and index finger as they performed beautiful pirouettes. Mara's garments were doused in rainwater. She tilted her head to face the bleeding sky, then receded away from the forceful water. She had felt nothing of the rain up until that moment. How could she not feel something so palpable? Unaware Mara was.

The late evening dimmed its overdue lights. Mara, still at the bus stop, showered in musty cold rainwater, plucked the leaves of a fuchsia bush, and played with them as though a game of solitaire. Each leaf lined up evenly against the eroded sidewalk.

Although she could not feel how frigid her body was, her limbs were becoming unresponsive. Everything slowly shut down, leaving her shivering on the bench. She mimicked the pill bugs circling around her as she coiled herself to remain warm. An intense fatigue settled within her, and she closed her eyes.

"Miss—Oh! Is she conscious?"

"Her body is extremely stiff, and she's drenched in water."

"We can't leave her here. Maybe she was waiting for the bus to come?"

"How do we go about this? Go tap her on the shoulder. Hurry, the driver is anxious to leave!"

"Why should I?"

"Say we leave her trembling on the sidewalk. If anything were to happen to her, a fraction of it would be on us. Just raise your voice near her face so that she's able to hear you."

"Michael, what if she's dead? We could be held as witnesses!"

Mara jerked her head up, inciting the pedestrians to rush their decision.

"Hello! Are you feeling well?"

Mara listened to the voices of the men and pivoted her head toward them, still half asleep. "I'm alright. Has the bus arrived?" Mara sat up, struggling to regain her strength and perception of balance.

"We were waiting for you to regain some sort of consciousness. Thank goodness! You must be cold—it's really chilly this evening. Do you need anything?"

"Thank you, I'm fine. Let us board the bus. Where does it take us? I will await the final destination." Mara stepped into the vehicle.

"Norfolk, a few hours north," the driver said. "The trip will cost. Luckily for you, Michael has paid it off."

Mara settled into a seat in the back. Three men wearing thick overcoats sat in the final row. One read an article, his hair parted perfectly down the middle; he held a toothpick between his lips.

Does one lose a part of themselves if the loss is only monetary or materialistic? Should there be any loss if it is artificial? A dying crow falls in the pile of man's wealth. He squawks, advocating his sayings, and yet all turn to face the direction of the money. They ignore what is not of interest to them. In life, women preach their perspectives of feminism, rights to equality, and various forms of advocacy in which their heart longs for. If noise is all that emerges, who cares to listen? What humanity does not see is that their voices are muted by those who are unaffected. Nothing changes since minds are unaltered.

Society does not like the middle ground as the middle ground is seen as losing, but how do you lose when you have gained even a little as opposed to rejected it all?

The man traced circles around the text in his journal. There was such a force in his actions, one could tell he was troubled. The curtains of his hair shielded the emotion on his face. Mara sensed a grudge. *Hope is the source that deceives us into putting our all into anything. Expectation for something to turn out in our favor results in such strong emotion.*

The man's heart pounded rapidly against the overcoat that sheltered him from the outside world, his fingers trembled as they circled the sentences.

"Sir, what are you circling so aggressively on that page? I'm curious. You don't mind me asking, do you? I'm Mara."

"Sorry. I'm just in my head. A lot of old feelings are coming to the surface. Broken promises, I guess. I'm Charles."

"Anything specific? I've dealt with my fair share of broken promises."

"It's really nothing."

He seemed to struggle for words after locking eyes with Mara. There was pressure behind her gaze. She was invested and had all the time in the world to wait. He sighed. "Have you ever been in love?"

Such a direct question.

The man gave her a sharp glance and briefly paused before saying, "But your selfish interests caused you to lose the person?"

"I'm not sure I have ever been in love at all. I have never experienced this mind-altering emotion they speak of in novels. Let alone the sacrifice of it. The intensity of it seems unreal. Why would anyone hold any other emotion higher than that of love? Or pursue any other experience when the greatest experience of all is in your hands? Have you gone through such a thing?"

He grunted, hoping to provide an answer with silence, but Mara didn't take her eyes off him. *We have only just begun.*

CHAPTER 20

"A year ago, I was engaged to the most loving woman in the world. She supported me in every way when I wasn't able to support myself. The problem wasn't her inability to love me, the problem was that I was never satisfied. My life wasn't enough for me. I needed a change, a way out of the conventional lifestyle. So I packed my bags and went on with my life. I threw out the years of consistent loving I was offered, and I left the state. Months later, I was able to come to terms with the fact that I was brainless for doing what I had done. If anything, I was extremely unhappy at that point. Then again, you can't truly appreciate happiness if you don't know what the other side of the spectrum looks like. Anyway, I tried reaching out. She's with someone new. In her words, 'someone ready to appreciate her and excited to settle down.' A few days ago, I came across letters she had sent me when I decided to leave and realized how hard it was reading her promise that she's going to wait for me. It was even harder to come to terms with her loving someone else."

People are drugs as well. They allow us to feel highs that are not possible alone, causing dependency. What is there to live for in life when you know the outcome of each step? What joy is there to look forward to once that joy has been attained? True joy only manifests itself in the imagination of one's wished destiny. What is there to look forward to after? Nothing. Life is detained by the solitary string of this supposed joy, until the burdens tied to it are too great, causing it to snap. Wishing to know more, Mara whispered, "Instead of ignorantly stabbing yourself in the heart by reading those outdated letters, think about what you want to do next."

The lights in the bus were turned off, for it was late. The two men across the aisle had already drifted to sleep.

"She's already gone. I need to remember that this

wasn't on her. It was on me. I wish I was able to see this a year ago."

Mara sighed. "Are you aware of the concept of change? More specifically, human change? Charles, what do you perceive to be the reason behind why we change? Personally, mentally, and externally?"

"Experience? Outcome? Fear? Acceptance? I mean there is so much."

Mara moved closer to the edge of her seat. "Of course, they're all valid reasons. But have you ever tried to specify with less of a general term? What do all of your reasons have in common, Charles?"

He ruminated on the idea for a few seconds, but Mara's impatience grew. "Other humans, Charles. You cannot run from the judges, nor from their effects of languish and eminence. If you were to run through each of your vices, at least those you consider vices, who incited you to believe they were wrong? The only reason I mention this is because the reason you bleed comes from her changing you. Your morals are not the same as they were a year ago today. What would your past love tell you to do in this case? Would you continue hurting yourself? I believe you should approach her in person. If not, allow her to be at peace and find yours as well."

He opened his mouth for a second as though ready to contradict her.

"Charles, she's already gone. Is she not? Make a decision quickly. Time pursues you, don't get comfortable in your sadness. Goodness, mankind is a lost cause." Mara squinted and turned to the window on her other side to rest.

"Mara, but she's gone—"

"For pity's sake! You mindless lover, she's alive! She's alive! But what is left to do? You either return to her now in hopes of reigniting what you had, or you let it be. If you give up now, however, you'll never feel the warmth of her skin, the rebellion between loving her and pushing her away. Tell me I'm wrong, Charles! And my purpose is not to trigger this unnecessary revival of ache but to show you the reality of your current situation. So stop," Mara reclined, "because your options have been laid out clearly. I'm going to rest for a while. Wake me when your answer clears as well."

Sirens and honking drifted by Mara's head pressed against the window. The noise reverberated against her skull. The roughness of the bus seats left the bottoms of her thighs raw and dusted with cloth. She could not fall asleep, but she played it off while Charles wrecked his brains to find an answer before the timer rang. So in her solitude, Mara let her fear gain its handle. Had she thought out her own situation thoroughly? Her knees were weak at the notion of self support and a life on her own. Regardless of strength, she knew her abilities and prerequisites were not enough to succeed. To believe otherwise was foolish. *To build ego before comfort is complete idiocy.* Perhaps Mara would escape for a few days, then return to Camber and Damian. She would forget the circumstances that brought her to leave in the first place. The built-up change and ruffled bills were enough to fend her through the week.

"Miss!"

"Yes?" Mara turned to Charles and grinned.

"If I speak to her and she genuinely wants nothing to do with me anymore, what do I do next? What do I dedicate my life to when all I've wanted the last few weeks was to go back to how things were?"

"Charles, murderers are not the only ones to use their rage to accomplish their objectives. Every artist of their own utilizes it; however, there is a difference when releasing it, for anger without restraint leads only to failure. Musicians and painters must come to these terms on their own. You are going to need to heal in a manner that releases rage positively. Charles, what separates a world-class piece of abstract art from child's art? Patience, the patience to grow, the patience of your hand's grip, touch, and motion. Patience. Now, you will not find what you look for overnight, but I urge you to return home and contemplate once more."

To Mara's surprise, the man stood. "Bus driver! I regret my decision. I want to go home. I'll pay you for the way back, I don't care. I'll wait for you to finish the rest of your stops first. Please!"

Do I dare to? Do I dare to join him and return to the stability I already own? My cruelty comes in the form of leaving others before they have the chance to leave me. Mara loved Camber, and yet, she did not know what love was. Her child, she had failed to adore to the extent she should have. Camber and Damian were still at home, still oblivious to her decision. Unfaithful, she had not been, but how would she explain her reasoning? Mara could not leave them. "Sir! I must return as well. Take your time, but take pity on us, I beg, as we have changed our minds."

Charles turned to face Mara, and she nodded. Although he knew the sparks of desire, Mara still had yet to feel, and it killed her to not partake in each experience open to her in this world.

The man driving demonstrated no audible understanding, but he had surely heard.

CHAPTER 21

We are on our return to my Camber, my love, the child I bore months on end—we are returning to my lights! I cannot remember at once the reason I left my beautiful home, why did I ever dare to leave such Heaven? I wish to return to my once pleasant life. At least there I am safe from the outside world.

Our destination is before us, only seconds away. Hours had passed with aimless conversations between Mara and the curtain-haired man, reducing the dense time. The strands of hair covered Charles's flaws, waving when he expressed excitement, but remaining motionless from word to word.

The other men had left the bus a while ago, so Mara and Charles raised their voices, irritating the ears of their pitiable driver. Alas, they did manage to keep him awake with youthful cries and stories of gore, balancing wise and philosophical teachings with fables of monsters and creatures. Mara recounted Camber's notorious folk tale about malicious witches and foolish warlocks, and Charles created stories of his own.

Charles sat beside Mara, sparkling with initiative. *You know of those countless people who pursue an impossible chance to greatness from an old adage of fixed life, well, how often have we heard the success story? I think I'm lost again. Why can't I be one of those? I mean we have heard it happen before, but those men and women don't share anything in common that I have seen... Or at least noticed. No!*

"Mara, sometimes I feel like I'm two people. In the daytime, I'm free of almost all emotions. In the evenings, I think of all the mistakes I've made and all the people I've hurt. I start hating myself at night, and everything feels so much worse than it is."

Not knowing how to respond, Mara allowed words to flow on their own. "Charles, I believe that some greater power carries my pain and burdens during the day, preventing evil—darkness—from over-encumbering me; however, it tests me when there is a lack of light. It watches in the evenings, giving us a chance to hold the darkness in ourselves. Our mission is to make it to the mornings the same person we were, but enhanced. In music, in books, in any form of expression. We are always searching. Don't you want to hear lively poetry? You crave the depth of its misery, regret, dejection! Something to connect to, establish a link between their stories and yours. We all do. So we are building our own crisscrossed track, cement, sweat, tear, just to grow stronger and to connect. I'm not sure what I believe in. But what is so ordinary is the anecdote of love. Society searches for love, crying of its labor, but then once it fails, they cry of our reluctance to chase it again."

Charles shifted in his seat, "How do you know so much about it?"

"Do not think so much of me, I'm nothing really. My truths come from books and the little experiences I've had along the way. "

"Another question. Why do people take advantage of others?"

The victim is never myself...not anymore... How to

describe an idea so vague yet so obvious? "Fear. It's a craving and a fear. Who leaves the other first? Once you have been repeatedly in the position of doe, it scars, but morphs you. You learn to stop hoping for someone to hold. Soulmates don't exist, Charles." Mara faced him. "Please, do not waste your time searching for one. Some people don't want to be stopped nor wish for the same dreams as yours. You can't stop them." Gathering herself, Mara peered out the window and spurred from her topic of conversation. "Alas, people are born mad. Only time tells of their transitions, internally or externally. It is only instinct." She turned to face him again. "Charles, do you like games?"

"Yes, I do. I like the competition. Being able to prove myself worthy, you know?"

"Worthy of what?"

"Living. So I'm not a disappointment in everything I do. What do I live for if it isn't to become someone different from everyone else. As a kid I thought I was different from everyone else. When I rubbed my eyes, I saw rainbow circles floating around, and I would stare at them thinking that maybe I was a chosen one. Unfortunately, growing up really shows you how the universe doesn't give you the upper hand. You have to force yourself out of blending in."

"Everything has a reason. It is infinite. A game is about who wins, not about those who come in close. And such is life. There is absolutely no point in 'almost' nor is there any excuse for it. We have no imprint on this Earth you and I. Neither do over ninety-nine percent of living things that have trudged this land. Nothing we do in this life matters, Charles. So might as well take advantage of others. Why is it wrong? I'm tired! No one should be overworked on the imposed boundaries of wrong and right. Why do others have more power over myself than I do? I'm ill. Mentally, physically drained from being lost each second I'm conscious. This world killed me before my first breath. And I punish others because I'm sick of pretending to be sane."

The bus arrived as Mara spoke her final words. Pushing past the driver, she could barely move her limbs. Ever so numb, Mara made her way home.

CHAPTER 22

"Camber! I have returned! You will never guess what miserable, traumatizing occurrence has taken place. Damian? Camber?"

Camber came from behind the corner, his face in tears and frozen.

Had Mara done something to make him look at her as if she were a monster?

"You have a warrant out for your arrest, Mara. Agnes's family says you harmed her."

It is difficult to come to terms with the loss of oneself. If you lose such a thing, what else is there to your life? When certainty is parallel to doubt, the values that make your foundation mean nothing.

A few minutes later, three police officers escorted Mara out of her home. Much too exhausted to resist, she allowed herself to relax into their arms. It was almost comforting to have someone else guide her. To carry the weights of her burden. Her eyes remained shut until she reached her new destination and was transported into that familiar space.

The courtroom was silent. Mara sensed Camber and Damian behind her, yet not a sound came from either. They chained her to the seat; the cold metal consolidated her. Between the crowded jury, she saw her father. His face was defeated, but he managed a smile. Returning him one, Mara reclined her head and shut her eyes once more.

My life was dark from early on. The lights were useless, for even the discovery of electricity did not solve my eternal black hole.

I was a secluded soul. Ever since the age of six, I would recede from society to create my own world. Design it, perfect it, until one day it would become a sanctuary. My sanctuary. Away from the wicked outer world and those people who would only hurt me. I never tried to fit in, and as a result, I stuck as the odd one out. Criticized for being different. Sometimes accused of not even being human. Those that surrounded me enjoyed crushing my courage. But I had my own self to trust. I learned to communicate with my natural environment, instead of the socially unacceptable exterior world my body inhabited.

Now, many will say it is controversial to have a child dislike their parent, but I need not to prove them wrong. You have not lived as me. You have not hurt as me. You do not have my scars. You do not suffer from the mental abuse. The physical abuse. The constant overwhelmingness that entangles the cerebrum. I wish that you never shall, yet even then it is a shame. For you will never comprehend the shackles attached to my wings. Each step I take invites Lucifer along. And I have become like her. Like mother, like daughter. I have tried everything. I promise.

EPILOGUE

Camber's Final Journal Entry to Mara

Wilted, unwatered, unkept. I wither through the addiction. Smoke and foreign fumes keep my heart submerged. Romance, a concept so beautiful rooted beneath the mind-altering vines that blur its truth. Funneling tubes wrenched together to forge this false mentality. Blue, purple, red. Pills of crimson and sorrow.

A woman so complex, yet so captivating.

I remain curious.

Codependent.

Regardless, I love her.

She will be mine forever.

Possessive, twisted, or absurd, it is true. While she remains certain in her verdict, I remain certain in mine. If her will is to leave, leave. I remain grounded.

If her heart is no longer mine, my heart serves for us both. As it is hers and only hers. I await the possibility of her arrival. And then. Only then will I manifest the recollection of our love. Bringing flowers to our grave. To what was not, but could have been. What is not hers, but is fictionally mine.

Wilted, but watered and kept.

The soil of our love awaits.

Through distance, through darkness, through devotion.

Then devotion will lie beside me in death.

Us wilted, unwatered, and unkept.

    -C

ABOUT THE AUTHOR

Alexandra Elkhoury is a Palestinian-Lebanese author with a lifelong passion for reading and storytelling. Since discovering her love for classic literature at a very young age, she has channeled her emotions and experiences into writing. Her work primarily focuses on mental health, exploring its complexity and the many layers that shape human journeys. Beyond writing, Alexandra is an advocate for women's empowerment, using her voice to champion social causes. Through her heartfelt stories, Alexandra hopes to inspire readers to embrace vulnerability and engage with the nuanced realities of mental health and self-discovery.